Brutus Finds a Friend

Dyslexic Friendly Edition

Tiffany E. Boots

ISBN-13: 978-1-963272-22-2

Sheltering Tree. Earth, LLC
PO Box 973, Eagle Lake, FL 33839

ShelteringTreeMedia.com

What is a "Dyslexic Friendly" Book?

Sheltering Tree Media has taken steps to make our books more friendly for those who live with dyslexia. While the following principles will not make every book readable for every reader, it is our best effort to create products that encourage reading and to support all readers.

Throughout the book, we use a font named OpenDyslexic. This is a free font that is designed to help dyslexic readers distinguish each letter from the others. For more information about OpenDyslexic, how it differs from other fonts, and research behind the font, visit their website: www.opendyslexic.com.

The space between each word is increased (this is called *word spacing*). This helps better distinguish when one word ends and the next begins. The line spacing is greater than most common fonts (this is called *leading*). This all should help with readability.

Whenever possible, the text is Left-Aligned but it is not justified on the right side. Allowing the right side of a paragraph to remain *rough* keeps the word spacing consistent throughout.

Our Dyslexic Friendly books are printed on cream or ivory paper which is also thicker than the average book page. This minimizes the sharp contrast of black-on-white pages as well as bleedthrough of text from the previous page.

Finally, Sheltering Tree Media has made colored overlays available when you purchase a book through our online store. You can find these overlays at ShelteringTreeMedia.com/shop/dyslexic-friendly.

These are some of the principles we use to create a book as readable as possible to those living with dyslexia. Some may find this helpful; some may not. Please provide us with any insights you might have to improve our Dyslexic Friendly principles. We pray this will enable many to heighten their love for reading

DEDICATION

For my girls Syranity and Clarice.
You are the best parts of me.
May you be forever blessed.
You are forever loved.
Dream big, work hard and believe in
yourselves as much as
I believe in you both.

Behind the old red barn and over the grassy hill, a floppy-eared rabbit named Scrump lives under the roots of the tall oak tree.

One day, Scrump was bouncing through the grass at the edge of the barn when a puppy started chasing him. Scrump knew he had wandered too far from his tree, so he ran, and he ran as fast as his legs would let him.

The puppy kept chasing him. "Wait, wait!!" the puppy called to Scrump. "Please wait."

Scrump saw his tree and dove into his bunny hole under the roots.

The puppy tried to follow Scrump, but his head could not fit in the little rabbit hole. "Please Mr. Rabbit, come out. I don't want to hurt you."

The puppy pleaded, "I lost my new ball. Can you help me find it?"

Scrump could hear the sadness in the puppy's voice, so he poked his head out of his hole. The puppy was sitting with his head down with his ears had flopped over his eyes. Then a tear drop rolled off the puppy's nose and plopped on Scrump's head.

"Please don't cry," Scrump whispered. "I'll help you find your ball."

"You will?" The puppy sniffed.

"Yes, I will. I'm sorry I ran away. I was told that puppies are mean," said Scrump.

"I'm not mean," said the puppy. "I'm Brutus."

"Hi, Brutus, I'm Scrump." said Scrump. "Let's go find your ball."

So Scrump and Brutus

bounded off in search of

Brutus's new red ball.

They split up and circled

the barn but all they

found was each other.

They raced up one hill

and down the next.

They went under the

fence that circled the

pond.

They looked in the garden and by the tire swing.

"I give up," Brutus howled. "I will never find my new ball."

"Maybe we should rest for a minute. I'm kind of tired." Scrump sat in the shade of a big rock.

Brutus sighed and sniffed the air. "Wait, Wait. I think I smell it." Brutus started to run, leaving Scrump to chase after him.

Across the yard they ran, down the hill and past the barn to the edge of the forest where it was dark and scary.

When Brutus stopped, Scrump ran into him. Brutus yelped, "Help! It's got me."

Scrump tried to hide under Brutus. "What has you?" Scrump asked, looking out from under Brutus.

"I don't know," stammered Brutus, "but it has my legs."

"Your legs?" Scrump repeated. "No, I have your legs." Scrump let go of Brutus's legs and they both laughed.

"Why did you stop Brutus?" Scrump asked.

"I'm not allowed to go into the woods," Brutus answered. "But I can see my ball."

"I can get your ball,"

Scrump told Brutus. Then

he bounded off to get the

shiny red ball.

Brutus watched him

carefully just in case his

new friend needed help.

Soon Scrump returned to the edge of the woods, pushing the shiny red ball with his tiny pink nose. Brutus barked happily; his new friend got his ball!

They raced away from the woods and over the hill, to the side of the barn where the grass was cool and wet.

There they played tag and rolled the ball back and forth until they heard their moms calling. Brutus picked up his ball and said goodnight to Scrump.

Tomorrow they will play again.

ABOUT THE AUTHOR

Tif E. Boots wrote her first children's book as a birthday present for her daughter. Many years later it has been shared with her sister, cousins, classmates and now you.

Tif was raised in Marana, Arizona and was working concession stands at county fairs in Arizona and Michigan with her family until she graduated from Marana High School in 2000. She became a mother and correctional officer in 2004. She then moved to Nevada, Missouri with her family where she was blessed with her second daughter and fell into a career of nurse's assistant for Hospice.

Tif and her family relocated to Mulberry, Florida in 2017. In her free time, Tif can usually be found on the water or at amusement parks spending time with family and friends and simply enjoying the life that God has blessed her with.

ABOUT THE ILLUSTRATOR

Syranity Barker is an illustrator who has always had a love for art. She was born in Tucson, Arizona and eventually moved to central Florida where she graduated high school.

Syranity illustrated her love of drawing early in life; her family were great supporters of her passions and always made sure she had a variety of supplies and mediums. While still in high school, her work was entered in numerous art shows. She received the *City Commissioners Choice Award* for a mixed media portrait of her dog and has sold several pieces of her work.

Still fresh out of high school, Syranity works two jobs and illustrates professionally in her spare time. She is currently the in-house illustrator for *Sheltering Tree.Earth Publishing* and also promotes herself as a free-lance artist.

Syranity enjoys singing, skating, spending time with her friends and family, and creating her own characters and writing backstories for them.

Syranity aspires to become an art teacher and share her passion for drawing and self-expression with others.

DISCUSSION GUIDE FOR BOOK CLUBS,
JOURNALING, OR PERSONAL CONTEMPLATION

1. Where does Scrump live?

2. Why does Scrump run as fast as he can?

3. Why is the puppy chasing Scrump?

4. Why does the puppy start to cry?

5. What falls on Scrump's head when he poked his head out of the hole?

6. What does Brutus need help with?

7. What do they find when they split up to circle the barn?

8. Name two places they look for the ball.

9. What does Brutus smell when they stop to rest?

10. Where do they find the ball?

11. What gets Brutus when he stops at the edge of the woods?

12. Why does Brutus stop at the edge of the woods?

13. Who goes into the woods to get the ball?

14. Where do they go after getting the ball?

15. What do they do when
   the get back to the barn?

16. Bonus question--- What
   do you think they learned
   during their adventure?

Tif E. Boots' Books and Awards

Paperbacks and Kindle

A Misfit's Masks 978-1-946469-01-30

Brutus and the Relay Race 978-1-946469-01-78

Brutus Finds a Collar 978-1-946469-01-28

Brutus Finds a Friend 978-1-946469-01-22

Brutus Finds a Monster (available Autumn 2025)

Brutus Loses His Sniffer 978-1-946469-01-70

Charlie and the Scavenger Hunt 978-1-946469-01-71

Charlie's Tangle 978-1-946469-01-38

Scrump and Friends Go for a Swim
978-1-946469-01-49

Hardcovers

A Misfit's Masks 978-1-946469-01-31

Brutus and the Relay Race 978-1-946469-01-79

Charlie and the Scavenger Hunt 978-1-946469-01-87

Charlie's Tangle 978-1-946469-01-88

Scrump and Friends Go for a Swim
978-1-946469-01-86

Dyslexic Friendly – Typography by Rolland Kenneson

A Misfit's Masks 978-1-946469-01-118

Brutus and the Relay Race 978-1-946469-01-116

Brutus Finds a Collar 978-1-946469-01-111

Brutus Finds a Friend 978-1-946469-01-110

Brutus Finds a Monster 978-1-946469-01-117

    (available Autumn 2025)

Brutus Loses His Sniffer 978-1-946469-01-114

Charlie and the Scavenger Hunt 978-1-946469-01-115

Charlie's Tangle 978-1-946469-01-112

Scrump and Friends Go for a Swim

    978-1-946469-01-113

Translations into Other Languages

Bruto Trova un Amico Boots & Maria Rossi

    978-1-946469-01-54

Brutus Encontra um Amigo Boots & João Silva

    978-1-946469-01-55

Brutus Findet einen Freund Boots & Heidi Müller

    978-1-946469-01-47

Brutus finds a friend EngSpanFrench

    978-1-946469-01-48

Brutus Trouve un Ami Boots & Melanie Thizy

    978-1-946469-01-46

Brutus Encuentra un Amigo Boots & Gabriela Villarreal

978-1-946469-01-60

Brutus finds a friend EngSGaelFrench

978-1-946469-01-61

Brutus Finds Collar - Spanish/French

978-1-946469-01-42

Brutus Finds Collar - Spanish/Tagalog

978-1-946469-01-43

Brutus Vindt een Vriend Boots & Pieter De Jong

978-1-946469-01-41

All books are available through
ShelteringTreeMedia.com/shop
BootsBooks.net
Amazon.com
BarnesandNoble.com
as well as many fine bookstores

Awards

Charlie and the Scavenger Hunt

Brutus and the Relay Race

Scrump and Friends Go for a Swim

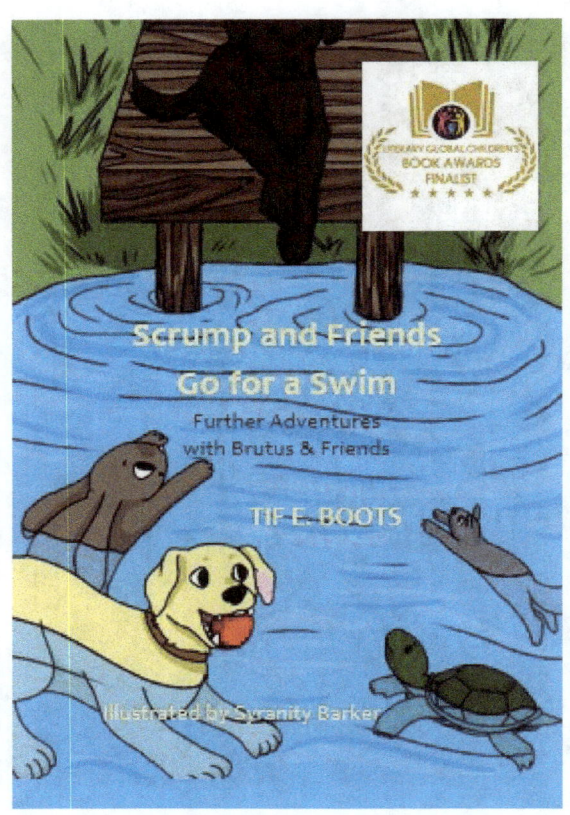

Brutus and the Relay Race

Charlie's Tangle

Charlie and the Scavenger Hunt

Brutus and the Relay Race

SHELTERING TREE

Earth
Publishing
ShelteringTreeMedia.com

www.ingramcontent.com/pod-product-compliance
Lightning Source LLC
Chambersburg PA
CBHW060755180626
46818CB00002B/580